Published by Sanderson

ISBN: 978-1-0690034-1-6

We are a question unanswered

A run-on sentence too long

A great ellipsis…

An em-dash in waiting

A never-ending story

FLORA BLUME

&

THE

BUCKET

OF

LOST

DREAMS

CRYSTAL ELIZABETH WESTMAN

TABLE OF CONTENTS

A Little Something from

The Author

After months of toiling away, this story's finally ready for your eyes to behold! Not because it's reached a point of perfection, by any means or standards, but quite the contrary——it has simply reached a point of no return. And I've accepted this. Sometimes you just have to let a story be what it is, take it or leave it.

Yet, I completely understand why there might be a kneejerk reaction from some people. I get why they might get a tad judgmental over how a person could ever think up such nonsense. But instead of getting all bent out of shape about it, I'm just going to dismiss this toxic negativity by giving these folks the ol' proverbial shrug while I secretly sneak away and pretend like I didn't write it. But as much as I may try to deny it, the truth is I did write it. *Yep, it was me alright.* So what I really should be telling you is this——while most of my characters have come from my own wild imagination,

I'll admit I've gone and borrowed stuff from my own life, and then I've blatantly stolen the rest from the lives of people I know; the lives of whom I shall not name of course. Mostly because I don't feel like being sued, yet more so because trying to remember the details of anyone's life, just makes me want to gauge my eyes out with Shakespearean rage. Besides, I couldn't remember the details of anyone's life even if I wanted to. So, somewhere between the truth and make-believe is where you'll find this story, while at the bar drinking some fine malt is where you'll find me.

Anyhow, as I was saying, there's always that moment when you finally let a story be, you resign yourself to what it is and then try to forget the truth altogether. And if that just made any sense to you— then you're in for a real treat, because in the following pages you'll find a whole lot of truth wrapped up in ONE GREAT BIG LIE. I've somehow meshed the two together hoping you won't be able to tell the difference.

Alright, let's wrap this up. For the record, if you think this will only be another story about a woman vying for a man's affection…well, you're most definitely sort of right about that. But in only seeing this aspect of the story, you'll be just merely skimming the surface. Go deeper.

This is SO much more than a binary love story about a damsel in distress. This is a story of magic, mystery, and most importantly—drugs, lots and lots of drugs and alcohol.

Just kidding.

Ω

INTRO

NUMBERS...

The Magically Inclined believe numbers hold the answers to the mysteries that be. Yet, if only they had taught me this sooner, say grade ten algebra, I probably would have paid more attention.

They often say things like, "if you see a number doubled-up, it's there to guide you, just follow the signs."

I don't know whether numbers are really there to guide us or not, but what I do know for certain is that numbers are extremely important to us as humans. A ton of people believe in lucky numbers, many have come up with numeric codes for the angels, numerologists use numbers to figure out our destiny, and then there are those who use numbers strictly for practical reasons and scientific reasoning. Hell, I'm sure if Einstein were here today, he'd probably have something witty to say like, "numbers? Why they're just a useful way of keeping track of the days of the week."

I won't dispute that logic. But I will chime in to say this, numbers are just these basic symbols we've created to fulfill an insatiable need to control and make sense of everything. I mean, if you really think about it, numbers are really just a bunch of symbols: our calendar system, the date, the time, the year, even the words we use to describe these symbols…are all just a bunch of symbols. That's all they are…a bunch of squiggly lines we've somehow made sense of and have all agreed to follow.

Well, actually we didn't get much choice in the matter, now did we. Society just dictates these symbols to be logical, common sense, fact. Take a second or two to think about how strange that is. We're the only species that gets these symbols. We're able to count on our fingers and toes for crying out loud, and then we can turn around and explain how we do this. We're able to create complex codes by drawing out squiggly lines and giving each of them meaning - now that's pretty damn remarkable.

So now all of this mumbo-jumbo just leads me to one conclusion — human beings have either inherited this systematic knowledge from somewhere or it's all entirely made-up.

Yep, I damn well said it, it's all make-believe.

The only thing we know for certain is that humans love creating systems.

Oh, how we love neat and tidy and logical things. For this reason alone it feels intuitive for us to trust in the systems we create. Heck, I'd even go as far as saying it's reasonable for us to want to trust in them — they're our systems - our symbols - so why wouldn't we trust them?

For most this means viewing numbers as the go-to symbols for fact checking, I'm talking your average scientist, mathematician, and your typical business associate. I'm calling these folks for lack of a better term, The Logically Inclined.

You've most likely heard a businessman say once or

twice in your life, mafia voice encouraged, "*it's all in the numbahs and the numbahs don't lie.*" That is to mean, people lie, numbers not so much.

Logically minded folk trust in numbers as though they are the omnipotent force behind all reasoning, yet somehow fail to recognize these systems as manmade. *We've made them up! We created them. They're pure fiction.* That's right, once again, we either made them up or extraterrestrials have implanted these systems in our heads to use at will.

And that is exactly the point — we created these ideas! Human beings. So, we should be allowed to use them however we want. We should be allowed to explore them as we see fit. This is not only true for the Logically Inclined, who use numbers to solve everything in an orderly systematic fashion, but also for those who use these symbols differently, such as The Magically Inclined, who use numbers as a source of divine guidance.

With that in mind, the most notable similarity The Logically and Magically Inclined share is this — an unwavering trust in numbers.

So, it seems like we all trust in these numeric symbols that are really just a bunch of abstract squiggly lines. Talk about lunacy, huh, but I digress…

Now, this leads me to magic. Well, actually, I'm not sure how it leads to magic exactly, but just go with it…

Ah yes, magic. Not the pull a rabbit out of your hat kind of magic, I'm talking the esoteric arts, the delicate dance with the great divine, an intuitive exchange with the universal forces that be. Magically Inclined folk often have a natural inclination towards trusting in the unknown, relying on sources of information the ancients have used since the beginning of time. But more to the point – they use numbers. They respect numeric codes as a sign of sacred perfection, as well as a source of divine guidance and intervention.

I suppose the true takeaway here is how both The Magically Inclined and the Logically Minded are all clearly just stumbling around together on this globe trying to make sense of a universe we haven't the slightest clue about. I'm talking the universe we currently reside in, the one our planet is floating around inside, alongside the other intricately placed planets we know barely anything about. And if you think we have the slightest clue, at least might I remind you of Pluto. Poor Pluto! The ill-fated planet turned non-planet, all within a single decade, stripped of its title, revoked of its status - scientists just upped and changed everything on us overnight and we're expected to believe we understand the universe.

You get the picture, the universe is a complex system, a computerized puzzle, and we barely have any of the pieces to put it together. Yet, this is the very reason, and most likely, why we love our systems so much, we love our numbers because they're the one thing we can point to definitively and say, *look, that right there is the truth, one plus one equals two.* Boy do we humans love it when we understand something. I'll just leave the whole, 'so *where do we go when we die*' question for another time.

All in all, numbers make sense to us. To trust in a number's significance is logical. The numeric system dictates the higher a number is the more value it holds. But to The Magically Inclined, when a number appears doubled-up, these numbers are to be regarded as the most precious, the most valuable, and the clearest sign that divine intervention is at hand. If you see these signs, take stock, you're seeing them for a reason. Basically, numbers are magic.

To give a better example of how you might interact with these numeric codes, let's say you see 2:22 on the clock, and you want to know if you should take that job offer that just came your way, well, The Magically Inclined would say take it, trust it. There's gotta be a reason behind that madness.

Now let's say your niece is born on April 4th, the fourth day of the fourth month, at 4:44 am. Now that seems meaningful. A coincidence? I think not. That's got to mean something. Maybe she's the next Jesus Christ in female form, who knows? One thing is for certain though, there's a reason behind it and you should probably see it through. GO FIND OUT WHAT THAT REASON IS.

You see, these magical numeric codes are hella old. The ancients used these codes to decipher the messages on offer to us, if only we'd stop and listen every once in a while, maybe we'd hear what they have to say.

This leads me to 11:11…

11:11 is supposed to be the most powerful and most magical among the lot. It's what I like to call The Mona Lisa of the numeric world, because it's always there, staring you down, following you around and creeping up on you when you least expect it. She's everywhere. You go to your local café and BAM, she's hanging beside a Picasso on the wall. You go into the bar for your morning bevy and SHMAM, she's there! A cheap knock-off hung between Jacky D and Mark (not the bartender but Makers Mark), and she's staring at YOU, always there and creepy AF. That's 11:11 for ya, and it won't leave me alone.

Everyone keeps telling me I should be relieved I see 11:11 all the time, that I should trust it's a good thing. It means I'm on the "right path" or something. It's the official sign I'm going in the right direction. That something BIG is just about to happen so I better pay attention. In other words, it's supposed to mean, just when you think you're lost, you're actually on the road to enlightenment. Though, I must warn against unrealistic expectations. If you're anything like me *being* directionally impaired, then I highly recommended using a GPS instead of divination, trust me, it'll just be faster. Anyways, you catch my drift… it's the universe saying, 'keep going, you got this.'

"Hells yeah I got this!" I yell to the dingy walls of my apartment (cause I ain't got no windows up in here to yell out of). My place is literally an office I've managed to turn into somewhat of an agreeable situation.

Let's see, there's a bathroom and free shower down the hall, which means no electricity bill or having to worry about buying toilet paper, that's the janitor's job. No need of thinking about heating in the winter, which is great because it's inching towards December by the second, and I sure as hell can't afford a heating bill in Canada. And then there's the liquor store conveniently located across the street. Ah yes, my one true love, liquor.

"I got this. I got this!"

That's me happy dancing around the middle of the room in circles. Though I'm sure a dog chasing its tail looks more coordinated

"I got this, don't I?"

Mm, okay maybe not so much. I have clearly lost it, my mind that is. Today was a total write-off. I spent the day sleeping. Well, first drinking and then sleeping…rolled myself a joint, smoked it, and now I guess you can say I'm, um, I'm——I've d-r-un-k a bit.

"Okay, I've been drinking!"

There's the truth hitting the glass of Canadian Club in my hands——both hands——like a child that can't hold onto its sippy cup.

"What? Adulting is hard."

It's been a whirlwind of a week, and I just want to sleep it all away. The last thing I can recall is all the shouting, the screaming, the books flying off the shelves, the dishes shattered upon the floor, and how Patrick never came home.

I've been pretty much lying around here for days. And the only thing on my mind is how I need to pack up his shit and get out. I need to run away. If I could walk straight, that is.

"I'm sorry officer, but **CAN YOU** walk straight?" I mumble to the imaginary man that looks a lot like me pointing at myself in the mirror. Tripping over myself, my bed catches my fall.

My computer's open from where I left off reading the latest. I'm stuck thinking of the next thing I should write for an update. How about? What's the adult version of running away from home? Asking for a friend. I literally laugh out loud after seeing the words hit the screen. Now, rolling over onto a crumpled bag of Cheetos I consumed for breakfast, the fluorescent orange smudges the white cotton spread and I seem shockingly cavalier. Instead of concerning myself with trivial details such as cleanliness, I have this urge to fling off my pajamas and lay here naked without recourse. Suddenly, my silk bottoms hit the floor and I am free.

A few moments go by...but I feel no more liberated than a bunch of chicks at a women's lib protest. Gosh, I'm getting antsy. I'm irritable and tired. Tired of everything, tired of cramped spaces, tired of the racket in this city, tired of all the traffic inside my head. But I'm mostly just tired of this apartment, *"I need to get the hell out of this mouse trap!"*

Instead of running out the door in the buff, I grab an abandoned milkcrate and start compiling all of Patrick's things...because that makes sense.

If you didn't already know milkcrates are great for compiling people's stuff. Cardboard boxes you say? No way—crates are solid, built to last. In fact, milk crates were scientifically designed to hold your ex's shitty things. I'm officially calling mine: The Bucket of Lost Dreams—a place where dreams go to die.

Here, in my most vulnerable state, *flesh against cotton against lost time*, I begin tossing in his books, his t-shirts, a pair of shoes, and that hat he always wears.

I honestly don't know where I'm taking his things but I'm sure I'll find somewhere to leave it. Maybe the lake's a good place to toss someone's crap.

"Hey, say goodbye to your precious things 'cause I'm tossing them in the lake like a body from The Mob, sayonara!" I shout, with additional splashing sounds to really let it sink in.

I pull on some mismatched socks under a long flowing dress, adding some dirty black boots over them to hide the faux pas, grab my milk crate, aka: The Bucket of Lost Dreams, and ready myself to exit.

I kick open the door with a,' Huh-Take-That!'

Between the back alley and the parking garage, I throw my hands to the sky and belt out lungs-deep my very best—FREEEEDOM! My boots hit the pavement and I'm gone.

CHAPTER ONE
THE BIRDS IN HIS EYES

11:11 PM

I am taking a walk…

Blackbirds soar gracefully among the trees, the forest behind me stands still. The crunching of branches and then darkness, silence is near. The black is all encompassing as my eyes adjust and I see the water bounce back off the shoreline. The lake is enchanting unto itself, with sand stuck to my shoes, I look up at the moon full of wonder. I stand peering out across the distance of my memories, staring out towards the horizon as I whisper to the waves, *"what am I doing?"*

"It will all make sense soon, Flora, keep on walking," they whisper back. My eyes light up. What the hell, I've never been able to conjure up a conversation with the waves before, why now? Did I really just hear the waves speak to me?"

"I must be hearing things."
I shove my hands into my pockets. My gloves are not exactly warm enough for this kind of weather. I poke around and feel a plastic baggie. *"Could it be?"*

Why yes it could! It was an old bag of the white stuff I forgot about (my darling cocaine). That'll warm me up. Did it the last time I was with Patrick. Maybe that's what caused all the fighting.

"Meh," I talk down the angel on my shoulder, pulling the baggie to my nose, I take a bump. I really can't remember the last time I felt so alone:
A lonesome so lonely, can only be felt within the veins of the lost and weary.
Terrible visions now taunt me
A ghost town's inside me
Every inch haunts me with your absence
Our bed left unmade
Pillows filled with dreams I once had

A tear rolls down my cheek as I try to breathe. It's chilly but in a calm summer's night kind of way. Uh oh, there's that awful pain re-emerging to the surface, it's been with me for days. I'm suddenly feeling the need to purge. My stomach is filling up with feelings. I don't want to feel anything anymore, make it stop! It feels like I've just been summoned to the electric chair but instead of worrying about my impending death, I reach for a razor to shave my legs. I'm about to die, yet my actions insist tomorrow's still gonna come. Though, when you know it won't – what you do next speaks volumes. I find a pen and paper in my purse and start to write.

MY BELOVED

I am currently taking a walk. I'd be lying if I said it didn't feel like you ripped my heart out and served it to me. I'd be lying if I said I wasn't hurt and saddened by our trajectory. I'd be lying if I said I didn't miss you. I never did care much for lying. The cold has now set in but still find myself taking walks along the pier—frost glazes its surface. We never know why we decide to take a walk or why we decide to end one when we do. How come we don't appreciate walks more? Maybe we would if we knew we'd never take that path again. How we rely solely on our memory to recall every Stop, turn, broken branch, dead-end. How we think staying on course means taking the same path repeatedly. Though along the same path, do the leaves not change, do the roads not need repair, will the cold not turn to warmth? Because as much as I'm enjoying these walks—I've realized I've never changed course—not ever. Not even once. Yet every day I still take a walk, the same walk— hoping today will be the day the frost disappears.

11:20 PM

I put down my pen to see the bus roll up just in time. Buses in this city always look like an advertisement on wheels for an anti-drug campaign, always lined with tacky crisis hotline ads. I've always thought they should just bring the doctors aboard! Hell, make it easy on the working class for once. I hop on. I don't know exactly where I'm going but trust I'll figure it out. I walk up to the bus driver and ask for a transfer, noticing the date it's hard to miss the obvious. I left my apartment just in time. I look down and the transfer reads November 11th, making today symbolic in some kind of way.

An explosion rumbles through my skull. That can't be right. But it's right on the nose, and if the theory bodes true, I must be going the right way. I decide to trust it. "I shall follow your perfection into the night!" I say aloud, storming to the back of the bus to sit by the window, I put my feet up on the seat across from me like it's a five-star lounge.

A bunch of drunken college kids are screaming obnoxiously at one another, an old man is talking to himself in the corner, and I start to think I'm not really in the mood for entertainment.

Just before the doors close, I make a last-minute decision and change direction—motioning forward, I lunge towards the doors – quickly throwing myself out of the moving vehicle.

Seeing the doors slam behind, I give it a moment of regret, "ah, such is life," now I have to keep walking.

Walking is better anyways, much healthier if you ask me. Yet, if there was only a doctor around, I could get that second opinion.

Now, here I am strolling through The Beaches. Just taking a walk, just a stroll on the boardwalk at the break of midnight, not that drunk, not that stoned, and it's totally not weird I'm just carrying this milkcrate around.

Sarcasm prevails

I'm trying to distract myself from myself. From my internal voice, but my mind always wanders back to where it all began…back to Patrick.

THE ARGUMENT

The fight was about a trip we were planning to take. He was already in the middle of organizing another out of town but promised when he came back we'd go camping. It was the season for it and he was most excited about watching the birds. He was into that sort of thing, which I always thought to be an unusual interest for a city boy, as cities don't exactly scream nature. But the birds found their way into his psyche and straight into his heart, where they'd fly for him and only him…just another man bestowing his gaze upon a naked dance without shame. *"Oh, that man must have birds in his eyes,"* I'd always say.

In that particular moment, however, he was listless. The sparkle was gone. He seemed lethargic and drawn out, tired of being tired.

He was doing the dishes, and I was sipping my coffee when I asked him about our plans. He paused. There was a stall, a fatal lull, a great distance between us. I was buoying upon the St. Lawrence and he was just watching me float away. No hand reached out to save me. No love letter in a bottle. I was a sinking ship.

He looked over at me emoting drooping wisteria. I could sense what he was about to say.

"I'm not sure, babe, I might be really tired when I get back, so you wanna just wait till then to decide to go or not?"

I was ten steps ahead of him. Of course he would be

tired, and clearly I would understand that. It wasn't what he said that gave warning, it was how he said it that sounded the alarm. His resistance rattled me to my core. He must be planning his exit, I thought.

It was the beginning of the end. The fight escalated. He kept repeating himself, "let's just wait, Flora, will you just wait for me please?"

"Wait for what!" I hollered, "*waiting, I'm always waiting!*"

Needless to say, we never made the trip. The one I so badly wanted to go on with him. The thought of the two of us hot and sweaty, immersed in pine, all seemed so romantic and whimsical I could barely make out the fact we weren't going.

It's now been about a week since he left.

It feels like forever.

Taking out some leftover pot I've got stashed in my wallet, I lay it out on a bench and roll myself a Jay, within seconds all my troubles dissipate.

I'm now scribbling inside one of Patrick's books. The words ooze onto the page full of vulnerability, raw and gutted like an amphibian. An evocative image penetrates the mind…

In the foreground of a cluttered cerebral cortex, Lynard Skynard's Free Bird plays to the rhythm of a dozen blackbirds in flight, soaring across Patrick's pupil like the full moon on a starry night.

I recalled our last week together: the stress had set in like a deer that's just met its demise. He was all wide eyed and panicking—being overly dramatic about a delayed payment from a mural he had painted the year before.

That mural was equally representational of Patrick as an artist and also as a person. He was simultaneously funny and mysterious, mostly great qualities until you were one of the lucky few to be graced by his dark side. I guess you could say I was really lucky.

This mural situation was obviously stressful. And to have not much to show for it was making Patrick, to be quite frank, a complete and utter asshole. The need to pay the bills proved to be too much, a daunting task, one which made him emotionally unstable like a petulant child.

From this came many emotional outbursts and issues that even a therapist would find disturbing.

It was becoming clear Patrick couldn't think of anything else but how little money he was bringing in, how he wasn't getting paid on time, and how this dismal reality was just too much to manage.

Yet all I kept thinking about was how little attention he was paying me, *Stand by Your Man* has never really been my anthem.

The next thing I knew there were dishes on the floor and tears in our eyes. Then there was silence.

It was the kind of silence you hear just before a bomb drops, a dog's ears raise and you can sense something big is just about to happen. I instinctively knew something was going down, but what…couldn't tell ya. I only knew one word was pinching my every nerve — pandemonium. And just like that, it was war.

I can feel the moon now staring down.

"Jeez, easy there Mona."

It's judging me because it knows I'm high and doesn't approve. The magnetic pull is so strong I can't ignore it.

It aligns women's periods for crying out loud.

"I'm powerful too, Moon! I'm drunk with power! Heck, I got so much power it's coming out my ying yang!"

Or maybe I'm just drunk. So drunk in fact I forget about the people passing me by in their vehicles while I engage in a conversation with myself.

I look at the moon beaming down with a nurturing gaze that reminds me slightly of my mother and I immediately feel bad about what I just said. "Aw, I'm sorry. I didn't mean that!" Out of nowhere the sound of the wind comes whistling past my ears, *"hush now Flora, it'll be okay, keep on walking, come what may, come what may…"*

"Ah! What the hell was that?"

But I know what it was, I heard it loud and clear, it was The Wind and it was speaking to ME. It's clearly competing with The Moon for my affection

"Sorry Wind. Don't make me choose, I love you both!"

I'm now shouting like a mad woman, flailing my arms about in circles. Who says you need to leave the city to get close to nature? It is literally everywhere, and it is speaking to me!

I'm spinning and spinning and getting dizzier and dizzier

"Flora, snap out of it!"

My reflection in the store window tries scorning me into sobriety, "you're as high as a kite, get it together!"

"Don't forget drunk as a skunk, too!" I giggle back, chuckling like a giddy schoolgirl with a multiple personality disorder. My anxiety goes from a thousand to Zen in point zero seconds and what's left is the sensation of pure and utter bliss.

"Awe, that's better."

A burst of wind suddenly comes out of nowhere and smacks me in the face

"Okay, I deserved that."

12:30 PM

I am reeling through the video footage of my memory…playing back the last thing Patrick said before leaving…he was standing at the sink and he just stared at me dead cold and then asked me to wait. "Please just wait," he begged.

"WAIT FOR WHAT!" I yelled back. I was enraged. What the hell did he mean by wait for him? I'm always waiting…waiting in line at the grocery store, waiting to check out my books at the library, waiting for the light to turn green…for the next season of Witches of East End to be renewed. I need a bloody explanation, thank you very much!

I'm now looking down at the milkcrate with all of Patrick's stuff in it., "shoot, I completely forgot I was supposed to dump it in the lake."

It's getting really heavy, and I know I can't keep dragging all his things around like this. But I also realize I'm all the way down Queen and it would be a waste of time to turn around.

"Damn it, looks like you're coming with me, Bucket. Stupid Bucket Of Lost Dreams, lost hope, of total shite…"

For a moment I sulk into the void and envision us getting back together… until I come to my senses. I look up and hope the clouds will suddenly part and maybe offer some advice.

They don't.

I honestly haven't any idea what I'm doing, not an inkling. I've got no answer as to *why, when, or how*. All I know for certain is what I am doing right now, this very instant, and that is — I am taking a walk.

CHAPTER TWO

CURSED

Okay, the truth…I am a witch.

Ha, there I damn well said it. I've been in the broom closet for quite some time now. I know, I know, surprising for someone with so much doubt to believe in witchery, but I wish I could say it was a choice. As much as I wish I could just forget about all the magic and mystery of this arbitrary existence—I can't. I only wish I could shut the visions out and try to ignore the spells scrolled on the back of my eyelids, the ones burned into my mind's eye. Believe me I've tried and not a single spell has worked. I definitely inherited this lot. But even if I tried to ignore it, it'd follow me around like that damn 11:11 sign. It would taunt me until I surrendered. I can't escape, I'm Flora Blume: a natural sex magic mystic with serious past life fears of being burned, and I can no longer hide.

A few months earlier my visions were playing out for me like a Hollywood blockbuster. I couldn't escape this scene where I was standing in line at the beer store waiting for *Godot* to appear on the conveyor belt.

When he finally does appear he mumbles something real wise like, *"Flora, you need to trust your gut, what is it trying to tell you?"*

Only in this vision, I looked like the sweet and glamorous Anne Margaret, while Godot was obviously played by none other than Elvis himself, handsomely decked out in an old vintage suit and blue suede shoes.

Now, I understood what Godot was trying to say, yet all I really wanted to know was—where'd he find those sweet shoes and where could I get me some? Ok, back to my gut, what was it trying to tell me?
Well, it was saying one thing for damn certain—that I was cursed.

I had sensed it for months. I could feel the cast of daggers shooting out from every which way, but I couldn't put my finger on exactly who and where it was coming from. And I sure as hell couldn't make these claims without sufficient evidence. Saying you're being cursed sounds as crazy as a regular person saying witches exist. The only difference is that hexes actually *do exist*, trust me. But you still can't just go around claiming someone's hexed you without having any proof. It takes a lot of willpower and energy to curse someone. So whoever was doing the hexing would have needed a really substantial reason as to why they'd want to harm me. And as far as I could tell, I didn't have any enemies. I gave it a minute and then did what any Magically Inclined folk would do, I cast a damn spell. Oh, you betcha I did. There's nothing quite like a little truth spell to get ya some answers when you need 'em. So I worked a little magic and then BAM—the truth came.

I wanted to believe, as most would, that I was just having a serious bout of bad luck: a fall down the stairs, a rabid dog had just bit me, financial loss was on the horizon, followed by a series of blindsiding events I couldn't explain. But there were too many variables, way too many things to rule out the possibility of a curse. That someone was trying to mess up my entire existence. Something just didn't quite add up. And what do you do when numbers don't add up? You start recounting.

Why all this bad luck? I thought. What had I done to deserve this? The answer is still unclear. Though it was obvious someone absolutely knew what they were doing. A witch? *Why, yes.* But who exactly had yet to be revealed.

THE UNRAVELING

At this point in the story Patrick hadn't moved in with me yet. He was still vagrantly looking for places to crash instead of renting his own apartment.

Out of convenience, his friends would let him stay with them or he'd find a way to weasel his way into their space by occasionally offering to housesit. It also seemed he would extend this gesture of kindness and hospitality to his new love interest—me.

He invited me over to his new crash pad, luring me

into his lair without warning. I of course thought nothing of it…. Until I did.

As soon as I got up the stairs it would be to my horror to find signs of a witch everywhere.

I admit, it seemed unusual at first, but nothing too out of the ordinary. I had no reason to suspect any foul play. It was pure coincidence, I thought. I mean, it had to be, right? So, Patrick might know another witch, no big deal.

As I walked around the place, there were witchy things sprawled across the entire home: pictures, gemstones, incense, swords, and a bloody shrine for Pete's sake.

Somehow, Patrick never noticed a thing. It was all hidden under a veil of artistic expression. But what the average eye might simply mistake for décor, I knew better. Décor my arse! That's not Ikea, that's a handmade altar hiding behind that strategically placed vase of roses. And don't get me started on that candle!

Where was I and whose house was this? I wondered. My curiosity was peaking. Why did he bring me here, of all places? Why would he bring me to HER house?

Then again to my poor logic, he was always taking me to strange places, showing me around, introducing me to new people and such. So why would I have thought anything of it. Yet somehow, I did. Because I knew it didn't feel right. The math didn't quite add up, one plus one equals three?

Huh? That can't be right.

And I hated that I knew that.

You see—people lie—numbers not so much.

I knew I needed to listen to my gut right then, I knew I needed to trust the truth spell was working. So I just stayed there…hoping some clues would eventually appear.

But the answers took their sweet time.

Growing anxious as the night continued, I took it upon myself to start asking questions. I thought if the spell wasn't working then I'd just get the ball rolling…

Well, that proved to be a waiting game.

There I was, the patient in the waiting room anxiously awaiting the doctor's prognosis. Was something wrong, Doc, was I completely off base to worry?

The night came to a close and I ended up waiting a week before anything tangible came to light. Unsurprisingly, just when I managed to stop thinking about it, is when the answers finally showed up directly at my door. Magic can be very convenient this way, and boy was I was grateful for that, considering I hadn't showered in days. I definitely didn't want to leave my apartment any time soon. I had gone on one of my well-known benders where I locked myself in my room, turned off my phone, and Netflixed my anxiety away.

Thankfully, that morning I got a knock at the door.

It was Jessica who seemed very worried. She had come as the bearer of bad news and brought as much as a pack of smokes. This seemed oddly important, important enough for her to rush over after a party looking like Beyoncé on Special K to tell me this thing she needed me to know.

"Yeah, yeah I'm coming!" I yelled from my bed. Jessica was wearing her tight black dress she always wears when she wants to score, the kind that shows the world where her underwear line begins and ends.

It was eleven in the morning, the usual for the after-hours crowd.

"Flora! I gotta tell you something, and I don't think you're gonna like it," she said, twitching about to piss herself.

Hmm, I thought, something I'm not going to like, I wonder what that could be. I imagined myself being on a game show where I was forced to eat chocolate covered worms for a million dollars, but then I sensed what she was getting at. "Oh, gotcha, something I'm not going to like, sure, what's up?"

I eased into her frantic energy while I put on some tea. Alright, alright, for the sake of honesty here…it was tequila, not tea, but you get the picture, we had 'beverages.'

Anyway, I let her divulge the news from the night before.

She claimed she had allegedly seen Patrick riding the subway with some other woman (gasp). Only this woman was not his mother, and by the looks of it, she was clearly not his sister either.

"He had his arm around her, Flora, like he knew her pretty damn well. And then…oh and then…you're never going to believe this. He leaned in to kiss her! Can you bloody believe that?"

I could.

I did.

So there I was, getting exactly what I asked for, The Truth with a Capital T. And yet I wasn't exactly thrilled about it. No, in fact I was damn pissed. I was peeved, enraged, livid! But the only thing I could do was let my tears drop into my cup of tequila tea.

I spent the next day pacing my room. I was trying to decide how I was going to deal with this breach of trust. At first, strangling him was the obvious solution. But then I reconsidered, thought nah, Flora you gotta play it cool. Just relax and everything will boil over. *Yeah, my blood would boil over like his skull in my cauldron!*

I finally went with the wise decision to maintain my self-respect by completely ignoring the situation altogether. Instead of facing up to the truth, I went into a cleaning frenzy as a strange cathartic way to rid myself of the filth, the film of deceit that had been building up over time, just waiting for me to wash it away. My logic was that if I smudged all the bad vibes away, I could somehow just forget it ever happened.

But when that didn't work, I considered making a spell that would wipe away all traces of Patrick from my life altogether.

That didn't work either.

So then I retreated. I watched and re-watched Eternal Sunshine of a Spotless Mind with great enthusiasm until I realized the whole point of that movie was not about erasing the memory of our exes with a magic pill but how we should take a chance on love.

Well, as it turned out, the clear solution to my problem was much easier than anything I would have imagined. In the same way most people operate by asking a question and getting an answer…all I really had to do was ask Patrick a few basic questions and he just "magically" gave me all the pieces to the puzzle.

"So, whose house was that again?"

"Why were we there?

He wasn't all that hard to crack, just a little naïve about how much I already knew. But now I suddenly had all the information I needed in order to put out an arrest for an un-abiding, and harmful, Magically Inclined Witch.

Git out your matchsticks y'all, This witch deserves to burn!

I later understood this woman to be as factual as any number you could count—the other woman. *My heart sank.* I imagined being the embodiment of the Titanic would probably feel better. It'd certainly feel more pleasant than any drug or drink you could hand me right then, because at least the Titanic had a decent legacy. *What the hell did I have?*

I knew I wouldn't be remembered in some lengthy movie for my tragic fate. No, I'd probably be remembered as the girl who died choking on her Cheetos from Netflixing too hard, all because some jerk broke her heart. How pathetic. I wasn't thrilled about the truth at all and regretted ever having asked for it. The truth can be a hard pill to swallow, one that often ends up choking you in your sleep.

Had I been sleeping?

Were the answers right in front of my face the entire time. *One plus one equals…?*

Don't ask me why Patrick thought it was a good idea to bring me to that woman's house. Or why he did what most humans would consider the worst idea ever known to man. But he did and so it is done. It's a story to be told now as though it were fiction, a moment lost forever in time.

Moving forward, I didn't know what to do. For weeks, I couldn't really do anything else but drown my worries with whiskey and rage. And though I was thrilled with having proof of my impeccable intuition, I was also very much startled by its accuracy as well. High Priestess chills rattled my bones. In all my years of witchery, I had yet to come across another witch who actually wanted to hurt little ol' me. And though harm none is usually proper etiquette for most Magically

Inclined folk, I could tell I was dealing with a woman who'd stop at nothing until she got what she wanted. Be it a curse or a simple redirection of energy, she was making it known I was not welcome.

CURSES…

The thing about a curse nobody tells you is that it's all in your head, in the mind of the one who weaves it I mean. It takes a lot of thinking juice to get a cocktail just right. But with a little focus and mal intent, you never know what you can brew up.

In my case it was clear I was under someone's spell. I fell terribly sick with no doctor able to diagnose me. Then I had serious bouts of negative energy directed at me everywhere I went. But most significant were the terrifying nightmares I'd have, that kept repeating like an ongoing crusade with the mind. A group of women appeared to me floating above my bed, a coven who all clearly wanted to scare the bloody buhjeezus out of me. They just hovered, and when the moment seemed ripe, they attacked…violently holding me down, slitting my wrists to draw my blood, all while chanting something like, *"we've watched The Craft one too many times."*

Alright, so they didn't actually say that. What I believe they did say was, *"welcome to the family, we've been waiting for you."*

Eek, how spooky is that! I'm shuddering just thinking about it. They clearly weren't my family nor did they really want me to be part of theirs. What they were actually trying to do was scare me half to death.

Mission accomplished.

This is certainly one creepy way you can do that. But they could just as easily have called to tell me they knew what I did last summer while riddling off where I was and what I was wearing, to really drive the creep factor home.

Heck, she probably cursed me and then recursed me every day since she began her tyrannical crusade, just to make it stick. Hmm, I give it a few seconds of consideration while I roll myself another joint.

Nah, not possible. I'm a witch! I know how to fend-off power induced crap like hers.

But then again, why have so many bad things happened to me as of late?

I'm a bit fuzzy on the details as I try to recap exactly what went down. Okay, let's see here…

Okay, I was cursed, check, and then shortly after I placed a binding spell for protection, check, I then cast another spell check.

Oh, shit. I pause. I completely forgot I cast a third spell. How could I forget THAT? I must be going prematurely senile or smoking way too much pot.

So I cast a third spell. But not on her…. I cast the spell on Patrick.

Ah, that's right! I cast it on Patrick.

Now it's all coming together.

Just then, hitting me like a ton of bricks flailed at my face circa the sixteenth century, it suddenly dawns on me that she must have cast a spell as well. But not just any spell, it seems as though she cast the very same spell as me. The exact same spell. I think about it a sec…

"that's impossible." Alright, it's not impossible, but highly improbable. There are a million spells out there, a million! So how could we have cast the exact same one?

There were all those questions again, coming up and biting me in the ass.

I 've only heard myths of such nonsense, and most of it was pure hearsay. These were stories of spells backfiring in unimaginable ways, meant only to be cautionary tales for witches who shouldn't dare cast the same spell on a fellow sister.

So most witches never really worried about such things because there are so many spells to choose from, it's highly unlikely that the same spell would ever be cast on anyone at the exact same time.

But what can often be true with life can also be true with magic——chaos happens. And when it does, we either forfeit or we find a way to repair the damage…returning everything back to its natural order.

Well, I'm not prepared to forfeit.

I know this woman must have put a spell on me. But I never thought she'd put a spell on Patrick as well. And what especially never occurred to me, until now, is how two witches could cast the exact same spell on the exact same person: THE EXACT SAME SPELL! The double-whammy of all spells."

Oh, Flora, it sounds like you really done yourself in this time. The energy's been put out there now, there's nothing more you can do.

Question: What happens when two women cast the same spell on the same man—do they cancel each other out?

Answer: Brandy and Monica's 90's hit single, *The Boy is Mine,* makes its way back to the airwaves, and plays on repeat in shopping centers everywhere, until the day you die.

Now, you see, often when a witch works her magic, she must believe the forces of nature are with her. But when there's interference, such as in my case, the effects are altogether unpredictable. Because when two witches cast the very same spell on the very same person—directing the same energy out into the universe, what unfolds can only be left to the powers that be.

So, two wicked wonders now stand. I, Flora Blume, am in a witch-off with Florence Greene—MY NEMESIS.

CHAPTER THREE:
TWO WITCHES
WALK INTO A BAR

I knew she was out for the kill. In all honesty, I suspect she had been waiting for me for quite some time. Why else lay down a curse? She clearly had something, or someone to lose. She was playing for keeps. And I suppose she couldn't have known she'd be dealing with another witch. What were the odds. Luckily for me though, I knew exactly how to deal with her. So, after months of this back-and-forth energy exchange, I wanted to make it clear—I was here, and I intended to stay.

WE MET ONLY ONCE. How she found me I do not know. It was a rainy afternoon. Much like Patrick, the weather had no sign of letting up. All hope was gone—and so was he. He was missing in action and acting more unpredictable than ever. So I did what anyone does when life hands you lemons, I took those lemons and made some tequila. Down to the bar I went…

The King Edward was fancy, the whiskey cost twice as much as any bar on the eastside, but I was quickly taken by the wealthy façade of the place.

I sat down and paid up. All I can recall is being anxious that day. I could sense something big was about to go down, I just couldn't place what it was. When no more than two minutes later a mysterious woman entered the bar: black curly hair, sparkly eyes, and a scowl. It was FLORENCE. I knew it from the ugly written on her face.

She and I had never been formally introduced, and how she knew where to find me was beyond me. But if it was by pure accident, or chance, or whatever, it didn't matter. She was now standing in front of me and it was time to face the music. Well, in this case…the whiskey. The front lines were calling, was I ready to draw?

She sat down at the bar and ordered MY DRINK, a rail whiskey neat.

"That's my goddamn drink, *you witch*" I snarled. Then I turned around and ordered the exact same thing.

Two grown women on either side of the bar, with only one option at hand. I looked at her, she looked at me and it was settled—*we would duel.*

There we were dueling whiskeys like it was a spaghetti western on a Sunday afternoon. It may have been raining, but it was as clear as a sunny day that she was gunning for me. So, I just kept slinging them back one shot at a time.

"Another," I yelled.

"One more," she requested.

"Another, please!"

"Whiskey!"

"Shot!"

I threw the shot glass at the wall, hearing it shatter

"Shit," she began to look worried.

"Fuck,"

"I'm so—" she slurred.

"Not me!" I gleamed, sucking them back.

"Really?" She looked at me with despair.

"Totally smashed actually,"

"Yeah-me-too," she said.

slamming her glass onto the bar

"Okay, enough is enough!" I cried.

I couldn't take any more toxins if I were the Ocean itself, which was disappointing to say the least, alcohol has always been my strong suit. But I had eaten so little as a tic-tac that day and couldn't handle another drop.

"How dare she try to take my man and then take my whish-key ash-well?" I hiccupped.

I stared her down as I floated ever so gracefully towards the exit, attempting to catwalk myself out.

"EASY DOES IT, FLORA. JUST LIKE A CAT" I whispered loudly, *gesturing with my paw*

I was walking and she was staring.

The whole bar was staring actually because I don't think I was really whispering at all.

Assertive in my stance, I kept on…

Soon thereafter, I realized I wasn't actually doing the

catwalk either. No, I was doing The Moonwalk. How one mixes that up, I do not know.

As you probably realize, a catwalk is facing forwards like Tyra Banks on the runway. But instead of walking forward like a graceful, sexy, feline, I was stumbling backwards on my tippy toes towards the exit. I just wanted it to seem dramatic, so she'd never forget.

I'm sure she hasn't.

Yet it gets worse…I kept going, "okay, take one step back Flora, now the other one, and now spin fabulously around without her noticing I'm about to fall on my face."

Oh, she noticed.

There are a million horrible ways to describe my departure from the scene that day, and each way is equally humiliating. To complete my performance, I hollered out a final, "ha, in your face!" ending with a congratulatory dance at the door.

My work there was done. She left confused, and I left knowing I made myself heard, stumbling back to my place in a drunken haze. "Curse you Florence!"

I knew she had something cooking up her sleeve, I could smell it, I could taste it, I could feel it in my bones. But the only thing I could do was trust it'd all make sense soon enough.

It didn't.

CHAPTER FOUR
A FLOWER BLOOMS

Flora: Derived from the Latin root for flower.

Blume: A variant of the family name Bloom.

I, Flora Blume, was born to a carpenter and a witch. That is until my mother got sick. It came in like a riptide sweeping the ocean rug out from under us without warning. All the memories of a life once lived were now gone.

It is heartbreaking when you see someone you love loses everything they've lived for, memory serves as proof we once existed. But when that goes…what remains are the pieces of a story never fully told: broken moments, shattered secrets, questions without answers…

As for my father, some would say it was a broken heart that killed him. When my mother died, he also left. I say they were probably right.

I suppose this is precisely how I became whatever it is I am today: a lost soul, a magic mystic, a dreamer, a poet, a believer, but also very much a doubter, an addict—and not to mention, very, very lost.

THE NUMBER ELEVEN

Whoever said, "not all those who wander are lost" clearly have never met me. Because if they had, they'd know some people DO in fact wander because they are lost. And then there are people who unintentionally get lost while wandering. Hence the following story...

It found me in the most mysterious of places. Who knew Mexico would be where I'd have my first brush with ol' faithful.

We all took a few swigs of tequila, and the parade began. It felt like a beautiful summery day. It sure wasn't the cold blasting weather we were experiencing back home. I didn't even mind the continuous walking for hours in the warm sun, until it seemed to have no apparent end. Only after seeing the same tree for the eleventh time, it started to sink in—there may be no end.

It went on the whole day. I was walking around in the blistering sun without a clue as to what I was celebrating, or why there was so much beer. And if I didn't know any better, it looked as though we were going in big concentric circles, all leading us straight into the seventh circle of hell.

I can still hear the large crowds of people cheering us on. And if things didn't already seem odd enough, they were about to get real strange. They started throwing tupperware containers at us as an offering to some child saint.

Yes, you read that correctly, tupperware was flying overhead like grenades being hurled at us from every direction. It was bizarre and hurt like hell, especially when one hit you in the face.

But that was Mexico, and who was I to judge. I mean, have you ever stopped to think about the standard American Christmas? Flying sleighs, flying reindeer, a man sneaking down our chimneys and into our homes at night. In most cultures that's called breaking and entering, so who was I to make a mockery of a tradition such as this.

I got into the groove of the whole thing, dodging plastic, humming to the rhythmic tunes, when out of nowhere there was a sudden lull.

The crowd stopped moving, the music stopped playing, and everyone looked extremely confused. Something wasn't right. Panic began bubbling up in everyone, the domino effect kicked in.

If you've ever been around animals when humans are panicking, you know one thing for certain, chaos is about to break loose.

But before I could even try to ask what was going on, the horse in front of me paused. It let out a whinny. And then proceeded to back up onto my foot.

That's right, my teeny, tiny, human foot.

I then let out a cry of "What the F!" Which nobody really understood, but very quickly translated the universal expression on my face to mean, "she's hurt, help her!"

I then gracefully hobbled over to a stoop to sit for a few seconds where a group of kind and deeply concerned men examined me to make sure there was no damage.

It seemed I was fine. No broken bones.

I sat down for a while to let the shock wear off. I figured The Parade from Hell wasn't about to stop anytime soon, so I might as well take a breather. After all, it was to my understanding, parades usually continue in a linear fashion, so there was absolutely no reason why I would ever think otherwise.

WRONG

At that exact juncture, the parade spontaneously split itself in two, going opposite ways. It was like watching a centipede be squished in half, trying to save itself by squiggling away in opposite directions.

The only thing that entered my mind right then was how completely screwed I was. While the only thing I could actually do was try not to panic.

Oh, but panic I did. The fork in the road would inevitably leave me concerned as to which way I should go. And also wondering where my host family had gone. I was trying to ask in broken Spanish, "do I go left or right?"

Heck, all the intuition in the world could never have clued me into this.

"What kind of parade splits itself in two?"
I couldn't stop ranting because I was now lost. I was more lost than your favorite piece of jewelry, more lost than Julia Roberts looking for another bowl of pasta in Eat Pray Love, I was fucking lost…and in Mexico of all places. What's worse is that I didn't have a single thing on me because my host family advised me it was too dangerous to carry my purse anywhere. Of course that's exactly where I left their address—*good thinking, Flora.*

I then wandered aimlessly looking for a sign, a clue, anything to guide me in the right direction.

So, I did what any rational, reasonable, Magically Inclined person would do when they 're quite literally at a crossroads, I listened to my intuition, pulled out some weed and smoked a bit, and then I called upon the great goddess Hekate.

"Which way do I go?"

I didn't hear back from her right away, so I smoked some more.

Within seconds, she emerged before me in plain sight. But let's be clear here, she didn't appear in the way you might imagine, not out of thin air or from the heavens. No, She showed up symbolically as a sticker plastered to the glass of a store window.

"It was a sign!"

I wandered into the store where the owner was quietly whittling her thumbs, as I smiled and then self-consciously asked to use the phone, "tele-pho-no?"

My head nodding and pointing at the dusty phonebook stashed behind the counter
She nodded back and passed me the phone.

I got straight to dialing every single Perez in the phonebook, which was insane because there are thousands of Perez's in that town. But it was my only shot at getting out of there in one piece. So I dialed and kept dialing until I landed on *"bingo!"* And with nothing short of a miracle, *upon my eleventh try*, there was a familiar voice on the other end of the line.

"Holy hell it's them——only took eleven tries!" I shouted to the store clerk.

She just looked at me, winked, and let out an expression I had yet to learn, *"ownsay ownsay,"* she murmured, eleven-eleven, Pretending to understand her, I repeated the sound back to her like I knew what she was saying. I still didn't get it, so I tried figuring it out, but only after a thousand guesses went with, hmm, *that must mean something* like "good." Yeah, that makes sense.

Wrong.

I repeated the words again, grinning like an idiot, mouthing *once-once* at her like Donald Trump trying to get through a presidential speech.

After a few attempts I gave up, purchased some soda and called it a day. That was the end of that Spanish lesson.

I then silently waited for my host family to save me. When I finally got back into the city, my friend Hazel had been eagerly awaiting my return.

I attempted to use the expression I had just learned with her; to really prove I was trying to improve my Spanish. She said something along the lines of, "I'm heading out to a protest in a bit..." where I took the opportunity to respond with a good old fashioned *"ownsay ownsay"* to express my solidarity...

That was when she remarked, "what are you trying to say?"

I looked at her confused, "I'm trying to say that's good, or alright, in Spanish, no?

"Nah, dude, that means eleven-eleven" she tells me with a veil of mystique.

My face scrunched up like a child learning a new word for the first time as she repeated herself, "

I continued to stare at her blankly. I was tired and now she was trying to get me to do math.

"Don't tell me you don't know what that is. everybody knows what eleven-eleven is. Where've you been hiding, under a rock?"

After realizing I probably had been hiding under a rock, she then gave me her usual two-second explanation, tossed a cigarette in my direction, and took off out the door.

Ah, good ol' Hazel to leave me in the lurch. As soon as she left, I began looking it up online. I could never have imagined *eleven-eleven* being a thing so renowned that even an elderly shop lady knew about it before I did. But it was a thing alright. One quick Google search told me that—It was a BIG thing. Basically, it showed up out of nowhere one day and has been haunting me ever since.

CHAPTER FIVE
GYPSY WHISKEY

1:20 AM

In front of a worn-down apartment on Queen, East, appears a very large and hideous sign hanging in the window, a neon light screams out at me: Tarot Readings. The very plump lady who lives there can often be seen sweeping her walk as she awaits her next customer.

I scrounge my pockets searching for change.

"Don't you worry your pretty little head," she tells me.

She sees my eyes wandering around and tries to divert my attention back to the reading.

She brings out some tea and sits down.

Pouring some into my glass, I quickly notice it isn't steeped, there's no smoke rising from the pot. She looks at me wanting me to take a sip, gesturing at the cup as if to say, "drink up my pretty."

I can't help but wonder if it's poison. I try to appease her by putting the glass to my lips and taking a small sip.

Nothing happens, "whew—still alive!" I say out loud.

She looks surprised and confused by my reaction.

"No shit, Sherlock." Then she mumbles something in her mother tongue.

"I like you Gypsy Lady, we're cut from the same cloth you and I."

I take another sip, "wait a minute…this isn't tea!" swishing the words around, I'm trying to get a sense of what's in my mouth.

"I know…I'm the one who made it, Sherlock."

It seems it wasn't tea at all but rather some sort of glorious magical concoction, it was whiskey.

"My father was Irish, he taught me everything I know."

"Well, cheers to that! Booze totally makes up for this scam."

"Oh, you think this is a scam, do you? Why don't

you just drink that truth serum and we'll find out."

Well, I can't argue with the woman. If she wants me to drink…I must drink!

Shuffling the deck of cards, Gypsy asks me to cut it in half, and I wonder how exactly this serum's supposed to work,

"The whiskey gives a more honest reading," she reads my mind. I choose six cards and hope there's something in there about winning the lottery.
Her eyes shift and I can't tell if it's good or bad.

"Whud-you-see in there, Gypsy?"

I can now hear myself slurring. This serum is far too strong. I need water so I don't fall off my chair.

"Many women in these cards—you lesbian?" she asks me outright.

"Um, unfortunately not, why?"

"I see so many women and they are very angry at you. What did you do?"

"Oh-h-h-h THAT. I did nothing but fall in love with the wrong guy," I say with a tinge of resentment.

She looks very unnerved. Getting up, she walks

towards the kitchen, turning around to beckon me forth, "come this way."

Okay, ha, ha…right, guess I'm going into the kitchen now. This is probably how she kills me.

"Sit," she commands, pouring more truth serum into my glass. I may very well throw up if she continues on this way. Is that what she wants? my innards all over her kitchen floor. But I can't say no, it's free booze—I'm poor not stupid. Everybody knows when someone offers you free booze you take it.

She reaches above the refrigerator…slipping her hands inside a black velvet bag and pulls out a crystal ball.

"Gaze in silence," she tells me.

I do what she says.

"I see a woman. A witch," she says.

She gazes deeper, pauses, and then quickly stuffs the ball back into the velvet bag without a sound.

Why is she making that face? Coming closer she takes my hand and gives it to me straight, "this woman is trying to take something from you, Flora…"

I nod, yes, trying to grasp what she's saying, but I can't help but feel the alcohol churning in my stomach. I want to barf all over her pretty little table, with its pretty little flowers…directly into the pretty little sugar bowl next to it. But Gypsy keeps on going…

"Only you can give away your power. So don't."

"Don't give away my power…*got it.*"

I see her reach for my glass and I pounce to cover it before she can pour any more *truth* down my throat.

"No, no, I'm okay," I tell her. She's now turning into two gypsies before my eyes. My head's spinning REAL BAD. I need to get up but I can't move. Lifting my head ever so slightly, I see Gypsy looking down at me, "aw you're so nice, Gypsy," I say through sleep incased eyes as she puts me to bed. She leaves a bracelet on the nightstand for me. The number eleven has been engraved into its center, and I am incidentally shaken into clarity, rubbing my eyes to make sure I'm not seeing things. "Why is the number eleven on it?"

She smiles and says as clear as day, "eleven-eleven."

"Yeah, I see that. But why the number eleven, what

does it mean?"

"Where have you been hiding, under a rock?" She snorts laughingly.

"So I've been told."

CHAPTER SIX
THE AWAKENING

"Wake up sleepy head." Gypsy whips out a book for me, and begins to cite a brief passage, "two parts of man, each desiring his other half, came together and throwing their arms about one another, entwined in mutual embraces, longing to grow into one." Beautiful isn't it. It's Plato's Symposium.

Well, I'll be damned. She's not only a Gypsy but also a philosopher.

She looks over again to see me squinting. Then with little resistance asks, like she's pulling out the Freudian chair, "so what—or who—do you desire?"

"I dunno. Is that a rhetorical question?"

"Do you know what a rhetorical question is?"

"Yes?" Not so sure now.

"What are you attached to, Flora?"

"Nothing…"

"Wrong."

"How is that wrong! You asked me and I told you…nothing, no one."

"You're wrong."

"But I paid you. You're supposed to make me feel better about myself."

"Flora, you wouldn't be standing in my kitchen if you didn't have anything to learn. Now just be honest…what are some things you hold close? Things you're attached to but don't know why."

"Okay, I have to ask! Are you really a psychologist masquerading as a Gypsy? Because that would be mind-blowingly GENIUS…"

"No."

"Alright then…"

Biting my lip in complete and utter despair, not to mention discomfort, I feel extremely trapped between a question and an answer.

She doesn't give me time to respond.

"Well, first-off, what's in the milk crate? Why are you carrying that thing around? Perhaps the answer is in that box.

"Mm, thought about it and still I've got nothing," I say unconvincingly.

"You've been drunk since you arrived, Flora, I highly doubt that. Why are you still carrying it around?"

"Because it's Patrick's!" I blurt out.

Oh shit, she got me.

"And who is Patrick?"

"No one…"

"He's no one with a box of stuff?"

"Exactly…"

"Ah, I see."

"So how about you just throw it out?"

She grabs the crate from my hands.

"Hey, give it back!"

"Let me first tell you about what I saw when I gazed into that crystal ball."

I say nothing.

"The number ELEVEN."

I gasp in shock.

"Something tells me you've been seeing that number a lot lately. But something else tells me it has something to do with that box in your hands."

"I can assure you this milkcrate has very little to do with anything," I say angrily.

"Well, have you been seeing the number eleven a lot lately?"

"Yes—why?"

"You my dear, are in the very midst of a soul reunion.

"Ok then, sure. And what does my soul have to do with some milk crate?"

"It means that whoever you're carrying around with you is most likely there to assist you with the process."

"What process?"

"The process of awakening! Boy, you really are a lightweight, aren't you. Follow along!"

She then hands me the book entitled, Signs of Awakening.

"Add it to your pile of stuff and don't toss it until you're done reading it."

"Ah, who reads anymore?" I say sarcastically.

"You do."

Man, she comes at me with such quick wit.

"Ah gee, is this one of those books you get from AA meetings? Cuz you know, I've read it already…but thank you."

"It's sort of like those pamphlets but without all the guilt."

"*I'm too drunk for this*," I say.

"I know what I saw, your twin flame," she asserts.

"Man, you saw all that in my milk crate?"

"No, silly, inside the crystal ball."

"Excuse me, sorry, but this all just sounds plain dumb. A twin flame is what exactly?"

She looks at me a bit surprised I don't already know, then requests I open the book again. It feels suddenly like high school and this teacher's a real A-hole.

TWIN FLAMES

In essence, a Twin flame is a reflection of your very own soul within another body. This person ignites within us a degree of self-realization like no other, swooping in and showing us exactly who we are—the parts we fail to understand compel us to self-actualization. And from the very moment we meet them, a soul awakening begins.

"Wait. If you're implying that by me carrying around this milkcrate is the beginning of some pseudo-scientific enlightenment process, you're dead WRONG because I'm just about to toss this baby in the lake! "

"Why didn't you toss it out before coming here if you're so keen on getting rid of it?" She asks.

"Because, I dunno," I say with the demeanor of a child.

"This all means nothing to you now but that will soon change. Trust me," she says.

"I'm so confused by this exchange"

"Okay, Flora, I think we're done for now. Why don't you take that book with you, read it and find out more when you're ready. It may just help you get home in one piece."

"Well okay, it is getting late, Gypsy, I shall be on my

way," I say ready to pass out.

"Time is but a number, Flora. But then you know that already, don't you."

"Hey, THAT'S a rhetorical question."

Checking the clock it says it's almost two in the morning. With a twinkle in her eye, Gypsy takes a moment to share some final words before I go.

"Keep walking, Flora, and don't stop until the tide breaks."

"How cryptic, thank you."

Almost out the door, it occurs to me I never actually asked Gypsy her real name. But without even having to ask she just turns to me and says, *"you can call me Ms. Whiskey."* Then she picks up her broom and waves me on my way.

2:10 AM

Taking a seat on a bench to catch my breath, I begin ruffling through his box of things, I can't help but wander back to where it all began. How did I end up here? How did I end up with him in such a toxic mess?

79

Always running and chasing and running further away. I flip open Gypsy's book and my eyes magically land upon what I need to hear.

THE RUNNER AND THE CHASER

Your twin is here to awaken you, to put you back on a path of self-actualization, self-love, and soul reunion. How could Wile E. Coyote and the Roadrunner exist without the other? They go together as a duo, right. These two belonged together. Even with their games, and their very flawed dynamic, something about them still seemed perfectly intact—perfectly imperfect. Who knows, maybe they enjoyed the games. Maybe they were okay with the running and chasing. Heck, maybe that's how Wile. E. stayed so thin?

But what if I told you Wile E. and The Roadrunner are actually the same being in two different bodies. They are the same spirit, perpetuating a cycle of running and chasing, all because they recognize themselves within the other. Not only can they see themselves within the other - but they can also see their truest self - the darkest parts of themselves - along with all the ways their spirit has been mutually broken.

So, one runs while the other chases. One fights for their freedom, the other fights for their sanity. And they go back and forth like this until they realize they've always been whole, complete within themselves.

For those new to this awakening business, this dynamic can feel way too heavy. All you want to do is walk the other away instead of facing up to your personal demons. Wait, did I say walk? I mean run. You want to run away and fast. That comes with often breaking your relationship apart, throwing the allegorical glass to the ground, and shattering it all to hell. And so the glass gently breaks.

AFTER THE ARGUMENT

I'm now reevaluating our whole dynamic. I recall how after we had that fight, Patrick just took off. But what do you suppose I did.... I went straight to the bar. He ran while I chased scotch. In a drunken stupor, I was leaping over hurdles, flying over mountains, chasing him in the clouds. I remember I'd been downing whiskeys for hours when I finally got up to use the bathroom and accidentally toppled over my glass. Broken shards fell to the floor making a beautiful mosaic., "down she goes!" I bellowed.

I swept my hands over the small fractures of glass, gauging my finger. Blood oozed out over the tile as I smeared it across the floor.

"The Beauty in the Breaking, that's what I'm calling this masterpiece!" I was slurring, talking to anyone who'd listen. Sad and alone, lying down on the cold tiles, I wept until they brought a mop to dry my tears.
I couldn't understand how he could just push me away and run the other direction. I thought maybe that's just our dynamic—a left footed dance, an unsteady waltz.

I guess now I know.

CHAPTER SEVEN
BATHROOM STALLS

BARTENDERS

Bartenders are God. Be sure to be nice to your local bartender, they're the gatekeepers to infinite fun. They can be the window to your soul if you let them. They know things, mainly because they listen to things all day long. So your things should be better than the last guy's things. They are your ticket to your next drink and hold the power to cut you off without notice. One wrong word can get you tossed out with red tape smacked over your mouth in no time. Be nice to them. Tip them well. And you'll get on just fine.

Flora, walk normally now or he won't serve you, I instruct myself.

Of course, I walk right on up to the bartender and

start rambling, "it's so nice to see people embracing life in this fashion, not giving a damn about the rules or the law for that matter. I've always wanted bars to be open all night, and now I'm finally getting my wish!"

"Ask and you shall receive," he says all hot and Jesus-like.

Whoa, his eyes are blinding me with such holy ways. How is he that good looking? That should be illegal. You know, it's always the pretty ones who get to do whatever they want. That must be why he's running an after-hours.

"One whiskey, please," I order like the Queen of England, with my pinky finger curled upwards.

"One coming right up, my lady," he responds with a peasant's nod.

"Maybe it's my his resting-itch-bafe," I say to the man beside me who's no longer listening.

I try again, "resting-itch-fafe."

I see the bartender inching towards me. He is within such close proximity to my face I can smell his coffee breath.

Uh oh, he's coming really close now. Why is he leaning into me like that?

"Hey, you want some of this?"

His eyes shimmer and I can barely put a sentence together.

"What…some-of-you?" I ask slurring my words and pointing directly at his face.

He laughs.

"*No, of this.*"

He opens his palm to reveal a little white baggie.

I'm well aware of what little white baggies mean (no good) but I figure why not, I need to take the edge off.

Now I know what you're thinking…cocaine isn't going to make me sober. In fact, logically it'll just make me more messed up, but it will make me feel like I have everything under control and that's really all that matters.

"So, where to?" I ask.

"The bathroom," he says, beckoning me to follow him towards the back into a very tiny, very cramped, and extremely filthy bathroom stall.

"Classy," he says laughing, knowing damn well I'd screw him in a garbage dump if I had to.

I try to ignore the toilet bowl filled with urine and toilet paper lining the floor beneath us.

"Well I'm classy as fuck," I say, taking out some coke on a key to do a line.

"Name's Brian."

I can feel the heat rising. I know this feeling. I know what happens when I feel this feeling. This inescapable knowing

I am Not in Control Of My Body.

He gives me a look and I melt, "so-you-gonna-kiss-me-now-or-what?" I ask. He says nothing and pulls me in. Kissing me heavy, he throws me up against the bathroom stall. We last much longer than expected for a one-off

I'd call it a one-night stand but it's almost breakfast.

He and I come to a complete stop and I come to my senses. I am left figuring out what to do next. After such an intimate display of passion, I don't know whether I should thank him and bow out, or just make a run for it.

I decided not to run, but what comes next is ultimately shocking. Instead of engaging with Brian, caught up in the fact we just totally had sex: intercourse, coitus, did the deed, did it, I can't help but notice that my milkcrate has disappeared.

I am panicking.

And by panic, I mean completely freaking out.

I've now started a search party to which nobody is invited.

Brian is staring at me like the Mona the moon, watching me crawl across the bathroom floor like I was looking for a contact lens., only I have perfect 20/20 vision.

"What ye doing?" he asks.

He's now giving me a look, and I ignore him.

"Okay, I'll try not to wake the beast," he says sarcastically. Then he laughs in an-oh-I'm-so-hot-and-cool-demeanor.

I want so badly to answer him but I can't stop myself from becoming possessed. The only thought process running through my mind is MISSING CRATE ALERT!

$200 to whoever turns it in.

"What's so special about this crate of yours anyway?"

"Wouldn't you like to know?" I spew back with nothing but disdain—I was being punished…Patrick's things were gone!

I begin searching the bar, looking under bar stools and peoples feet, and behind every nook and cranny, until one very drunken dude appears out of nowhere, "hey, I hear you're the chick looking for a milk crate?"

"Yeah, that'd be me, why?" I look him up and down to see if he's hidden it under his jacket. But he hasn't.

"Yeah, well I saw it earlier and put it up somewhere so nobody would trip over it."

"You know where it is!" I ask enthusiastically.

"That's the thing, I can't remember exactly where I put it, um, maybe on top of the refrigerator?"

I stare at him in disbelief. But instead of judging this dimwit, I'm trying hard to focus.

"Now, if I were a milk crate, where would I be?"

I'm casing the joint like a professional thief.

I'm starting to think The Bucket of Lost Dreams is

one hundred percent accurate. It's all in the name.

All of my dreams are lost hiding inside that milk crate, somewhere inside this bar.

Brian appears YET AGAIN.

"Hey Hot Girl…I found your stuff!"

"First off, my name's Flora not Hot Girl. And you have my stuff—where?"

It's nowhere in sight, I'm starting to think he's lying. He's pointing over towards the kitchen to where a man suddenly flies through the swinging doors.

"It's in the oven. Josh put it in there so nobody would take it!"

"Did I just hear that right? MY MILKCRATE is seriously in the oven?"

I give him a curious look to make sure I wasn't confused, nope, not confused, it's in the oven, a big pizza oven to be exact.

"Well, now we're cooking," I joke, trying to make light of an infuriating situation.

I push through the crowd to go fetch my crate, looking for the nearest fire escape, that way I can duck out and won't have to say goodbye to Brian after our "intimate morning" together. Or maybe I can just avoid the whole thing and ghost?

Question: How does one suddenly become a ghost?

Answer: Don't answer that.

Scanning the room, he's nowhere to be found. So I quickly grab my jacket and lunge towards the nearest exit. But that is when I hear…

"Flora, wait!"

Ah, he's got me.

I try to swim away like a fish but my fins aren't working!

"I am swimming away, Brian!" I shout halfway out the door.

"Okay, sure, that's cool…" he says.

Ugh, he sounds like a surfer, so sarcastic and charming, the way hipsters sound when they're trying to impress you.

"Look, you are a cat that just wants to stalk its prey. But I am a fish, Brian, and cannot allow it. I must leave and never return."

His eyes widen like he's about to eat me. Instead he just asks, "hey maybe I can call ya sometime?"

How sweet, he's asking me out on a date after boning in the bathroom. How does one respond to that? This was my cue to run.

"Um, yeah, okay…sure!" I say, grabbing my stuff as I jet swiftly out the door. Turning to give him one final goodbye, I can think of nothing better to say than, "thanks for all the sexxx!"

The sky overhead is grey, and the clouds are starting to poof up like a child's face. You know, how they get all puffy when they're about to cry. I can hear the thunder in the distance, a storm's brewing. Dammit, what do I do now? And as fast as I can say "I'm screwed," it begins to pour.

CHAPTER 7

PART TWO: GOOGLE IS MAGIC

If there was ever proof magic existed, it would be Google. The fact that we can literally ask it any question, and then receive an answer, is by far the most comprehensive way to describe magic that I can think of.

Question: "What's my destiny?"

Answer: "Google it, dummy."

Scrolling through my phone, I'm receiving all kinds of epiphanies. Here I was thinking this walk was only about one thing (my breakup) when it's about so much more. This walk is about every single choice I've ever made.

And every person I've ever met. They were all there to teach me something, but I just ignored them. So many lessons I didn't want to learn. So many lessons about my addictions, my actions, my pain, my past. In my mind I was always the solution and never the problem. But here is the truth being laid out in front of me. Maybe I have been sleeping this whole time. And maybe I am just starting to wake up.

I always assumed I was the accomplice, Never the crook. Yet I am both. Equally good And just as bad. Like two accomplices in the night. Harboring the same secret. The same crime. The same regret.

I always thought I was on the right side of history, but never could admit when I wasn't. Never learning my lesson, always stuck in the same karmic loop. I've probably been repeating the same mistakes over and over for centuries. Patrick may be the runner in this situation—but who's been running away from themselves their entire life. Again—ME.

7:30 AM

I pick up my milkcrate and start the long trek home. I need to work towards getting clean. If only there was a spell for that. Heck, maybe there is a spell for that. Out of nowhere, I feel my entire body fly towards the ground. I try to use my hands to catch my fall but it's too late...I'm on the ground and there might be blood!

"Somebody HELP, I've been pushed by the wind!"

Then I hear a loud yell behind me, "move it, lady! Eleven times-ha-ha. You can't catch me!"

That number again, un-fucking-believable.

"Where is he going?"

I see him jog towards the Cathedral, up the stairs, and fly through the doors like a bird, or like a ghost...

"Do I see dead people?"

A police officer pushes me out of the way, "excuse me, officer coming through!" He yells, chasing the man at warp speed.

Okay, not a ghost then, phew.

I can see the man yelling from the stairs of the cathedral, "you can't catch me! I'm in a church. What you gonna do, arrest me in the house of God!"

Man's got a point.

The cops are reluctant to disturb the peace. They just stand and wait, expecting him to come down without a fight.

I'm rooting for this underdog, this champion of worlds, when suddenly I get the bright idea I can follow him in.

I hear an officer arguing over this man's whereabouts, *"you let him go into a Church! You know Fernandez is a nuisance, dammit."*

"I didn't mean to!" the other cop yells back.

I take this moment to find him.

"Where'd ye go, Ferny?"

I'm calling him like a dog.

Suddenly I see someone scoot down the back and fly into a room. I follow behind. We are now playing hide and seek, and Ferny has clearly met his match because I am a professional seeker.

"Leave me alone!" he yells.

I enter the room where I expect to find him scaling

the walls with his tentacles, but there is no tentacle goo sticking to the wall, just him kneeling under the desk with a cloak draped around him.

"I'm not going to hurt you, I promise," I say trying to reassure him.

"I wasn't born yesterday, who are you and what do you want?"

"I'm not going to hurt you. I just saw you running away from the cops and wanted to make sure you're okay."

"Well, I'm very okay, thanks lady, but don't need your help."

"Right, sorry. I'm just really *high* right now."
He's now undressing me with his eyes. And I actually consider taking my clothes off before I remember the police are looking for him. And now maybe they're looking for me too! Uh oh—the police are most definitely looking for me.

This leaves me no other option but to run like hell and take him with me.

Flora, why are you always an accomplice?

I take Fernandez's hand and we run like the wind, "don't worry I'm magic!" I tell him as we head out the back.

He's now staring at me like I'm the one who's mentally unwell.

"Sure lady…and I'm Elvis."

We encounter a fence where we start to climb. He lends me a hand to help me over with my milk crate, but when I toss it over some books fall out.

"Man, why'd you have to bring that wit-you? Feels like a hundred pounds."

"I don't think this is the time to get to know one another!" I shout, dangling over the side, nearly ripping my jacket on an open wire.

We continue down the alley and pause at the street corner. Now seeing a streetcar approaching, we jump aboard without a trace.

"We're free!" I yell out, slinking down into the seat.

"You don't have to duck, it's me they're after."

"If only you knew the crimes I've committed."

I can tell he's got a killer sense of humor. Or maybe he's just a killer with a good sense of humor?

I pause to consider the likelihood of that being true.

"Hey, did you kill someone?" I ask him outright like that's a perfectly normal question.

"UM NO, why did you kill someone?" He asks, backing away from me, which is fair since I did just insinuate he looks suspect for murder.

"Sorry, I say stupid things when I'm stoned."

"God damn, now I really need to get stoned." He says.

Maybe I've got something stashed. I'm searching my bag again, but still nothing.

"All out," I say.

He makes a sigh and then stretches his arms, "well, good thing I know someone who's good for it. And she lives right around the corner. Wanna take a field trip?"

NOTE TO SELF: this is an invitation from a criminal to join him at his friend's house, who is probably also a criminal, where they'll probably try and initiate me into their drug ring. I think about it a sec then unwittingly say, "sure let's go."

We walk a lot farther than just around the corner but

I'm cool with it, because all I can think about is getting high.

I'm feeling good about having connected with Fernandez, and for a second I consider taking him home to live with me. Can adults adopt other adults? That should totally be a thing.

At first glance the house looks beautiful. But getting a second glimpse, the door looks awfully familiar. And then it dawns on me why—I've been here before.

CHAPTER EIGHT
WITCHES WELCOME

From the door hangs a sign: Witches Welcome. It feels like a test in the house of horrors. Choose a door, any door! Which one's it gonna be! Where's it gonna lead to! The only problem is there's just one door. My mind's racing as I slowly begin inhaling my own self-loathing: "here I am, I give in, I can't win. I am the greatest loser, the most beautiful failure, the queen of giving up, the path of least resistance personified."

"You, okay?" Ferny asks, checking while I have a full-on conversation with myself. I try to shake off the shock, but I just can't—I realize I am standing at Florence's Door. I can't stop staring at it. I feel like I'm standing at a corner with two bus routes that cross each other. You know how it goes, you're standing at an intersection and you have two buses you could take. Which one do you choose?

"FLORENCE'S DOOR!"

Fernandez is now officially freaked out, "whoa, you can see who's standing behind the door? That's spooky shit man," he's staring at me like I'm a prophet.

"No, I've been here before," I shout back.

"You mean you've been here before… *in your mind?*"

He shoots me an eerie stare.

"No in real life!"

I'm becoming more and more frustrated each second I continue to stand at her doorstep.

"Wait! You actually know Florence? Wow, what are the odds of that?"

He's about to high-five me but I leave him hanging.

"Zero odds," I mutter.

"She's cool shit man. But I think maybe she's not home. Let me call her friend to see if he's there, he sometimes comes to the door."

"Fernandez, back away from the phone this instant."

He's looking at me uneasy. But then just shrugs, waiting for me to provide a better solution to our little drug problem.

I say nothing and he buckles, "look, we're here now and we want drugs! So I don't see why we should leave only to turn around and come back?"

"Because I'm NOT coming back, that's why. Not going in there either. Not now, not ever!"

Yep, I'm screaming like a crazy person and Ferny's not having any of it.

"What the flying fuh-doo is wrong with you?"

"One: A flying fuh-doo is not a thing! And Two: I am not entering that house. No way. No how. You're on your own buddy."

"Number one," he laughs. "how are we going to pay for all the drugs?"

"Well, you'll have to figure that out for yourself."

"Man, you are a witch. But replace the double-u with a big fat B!"

"Ha, funny…"

He might think I'm being a total B.I.T.C.H, but he doesn't know how weird this is. It is totally weird. The universe is playing a big fat joke on me and I'm not in the mood for comedy right now. What's worse is that I am standing here holding a milkcrate full of Patrick's stuff.

Maybe it was all supposed to happen this way. Maybe I am supposed to go give it back to him here. Or maybe I'm just supposed to hand it over to Florence. *Ouch, that would sting*. Here's all Patrick's stuff, you can have him along with it.

Here I am, griping and moaning while digging my heels into Florence's front lawn. Fernandez is on his phone texting someone. I'm pretty sure it's her, or even worse, Patrick.

What if Patrick is upstairs? Should I go up to find out?

You know what they say about there never being a bad question? Well, there are bad questions. There are things you should never ask, and things you never want to know. So, now here I stand, faced with this stupid door, just as I remember it: wooden and begging for me to open. *Which one's it gonna be! Where's it gonna lead to!*

"Okay, it turns out she's home. She said you're more than welcome to come in," he says, referring to Florence.

"What the hell? Why would she want that!"

Ugh, how did this happen? I feel completely defeated. I feel like crying, or smashing something, whichever comes first.

Fernandez is growing impatient, declaring he's going to leave me behind: One troop down! I have to keep moving, Lieutenant!

He walks towards the door, turns the knob slowly, and with a gentle tone of voice, he accepts his defeat, "okay, I'm going in. Feel free to stand there all day if you want, but I might be a while."

I'm becoming ever so aware of my rapid heartbeat as I start counting backwards.

I can't help but think if Patrick and I are supposed to meet here then so be it. But I honestly cannot accept this reunion under these circumstances. In a moment of fight or flight I try to remember what Gypsy said about owning my power. I am powerful. I am strong. I am fearless. And I AM DONE.

Before I even make it from Florence's front door to the sidewalk, I realize throwing his things out is probably a terrible idea. I know I'd want to have my stuff back in proper condition

With the milkcrate to my chest, I walk it to the front door of its memorial *Singing the death march*

I place the milkcrate filled with Patrick's things upon Florence's doorstep and utter some final last words, "it was nice knowing you milk crate. It was the best of times, it was the worst of times. But now it is time for us to part. I'm leaving you here where Patrick will find you. *Goodbye.*"

FIXING THE FIX

I am walking towards the beach, which is only a short distance away. Walking a few blocks south where I can see the water now come into my eyeline, I start to consider what I'm supposed to do next. I know I am an addict. I need help. I wish I could just wash the past away but I can't. I think I'm ready to accept I need to get clean.

Question: How do I get clean?

Answer: Take a shower

There are no guarantees in this life. The only thing we've really got is hope. We hope the bus will show up on time, that everyone will do what they say they will, that your waiter doesn't spit in your food. We hope the sun will still rise tomorrow. And that tomorrow will eventually come.

But when you know for certain it's not coming—what you do next speaks volumes.

WHERE IS PATRICK?

Patrick is waking up to the sound of birds chirping at his windowsill. He walks down the hallway to the bathroom, turns on CBC and runs himself a hot bath. He then makes himself a fresh pot of coffee while waiting for the tub to fill, he receives a text.

FLORENCE: hey, some chick dropped your stuff off.

Wanna come pick it up?

He finds it sensible to stop by to get his stuff before heading down to the beach. He steps quickly inside and sees a milkcrate sitting in the hall. He immediately realizes who must have dropped it off. Rustling through his stuff, he comes across a book that isn't actually his, it has a lovely warmhearted note attached to the front: Happy Fucking Birthday! Luv, Flora, xo

He realizes Flora must have bought it for him and never gave it to him. He locks his bike to a tree out front, and then walks down to the beach with his milkcrate tucked under one arm, wondering about Flora and how she got his stuff to Florence's in the first place. Yet, as quickly as this thought entered his mind, it left just as fast. Because all he wanted to do was take a walk.

He unravels his brand-new kite. Unwinding the string wrapped in a ball, he releases it to the wind and decides this will be the day that changes his entire life.

CHAPTER NINE

HOW DO YOU END A WALK?

9:00 AM

There are so many reasons why I decided to take a walk. But how to end it is the question. I can't help but ask, when is the journey done? Is it finished when I reach a particular point and decide it's done, or does it end the same way you end a sentence, by putting a period at the end and calling it a day. I'm not so sure when to call it quits, I usually just have somewhere else to be. If you had nowhere else to go, would you keep on walking? I'm starting to wonder if I'm ever going to make it home.

THE ODYSSEY

The Odyssey was certainly all about being on this epic adventure. [i] But let us consider for a moment the possibility that Odysseus was never planning on being away so long. Maybe he was just stepping out to get some air and got distracted. Heck, maybe he was just taking a walk.

What we know for certain is that he was heading home (a pending thought right about now). All Odysseus really wanted was to return home to his wife. I suppose that incentive made it easier for him to find his way.

The irony of going home, though, is you don't really have to go anywhere to feel like it's far away. You could be perfectly seated upon your couch and still feel as homeless as my pal Fernandez. Home is so much more than a roof over your head. It's a feeling. It's a place you feel safe. It's where you feel you belong.

I imagine myself being back in my cramped apartment, tucked into bed. And it dawns on me that maybe my bed is my home, ah, bed. I wonder if Odysseus ever felt homesick for his bed. Though, I'm sure being stranded on that island with that nymph was pretty comforting. Not exactly a burden if you know what I mean.

But in the end, the only thing Odysseus really wanted was to go home. He wanted to get back so he could sleep with his wife (go figure). In fact, he wanted to be with his wife so much, he fought an entire army of suitors for her. Now, what woman wouldn't have wanted that?

Question: You know what I would have fought for?

Answer: My bed

9:30 AM

The water is crashing on the shore. I can feel the November chill setting in, but it feels eerily warm for this time of year, global warming has arrived. I am passing in and out of consciousness as I lay my head upon the sand, drifting away to the rhythm of the waves. Gravity pulls me down and tucks me in. I doze off to its melody…

"What the hell, can't you see me lying here?"

"Yes, and you are very beautiful sleeping here, I must say hello."

His accent is so charming. After the night I've had, I'm not sure if this dude is just scruffy or homeless. What are the chances I attract two homeless men in one night? Instead, he pulls out a tab of acid with my name on it. He ingests some then hands me a few pieces to chew.

"Here is the best acid in zee world."

"Ah, dammit, just as I'm about to get clean you hand me the world's best acid!"

This is a tough one. I know I'm supposed to decline his offer but I'm just so tired, and I know it will keep me awake, and will possibly be the last time I ever do any drugs again. Besides, if I'm going to get to fixing things, it's not going to be today.

I give in, "ah, well, tomorrow's another day," I say, taking and licking the magical tab. I'll get clean tomorrow."

Time slows down. Every inch of me is pulsating. I can't feel my face. He stares into my eyes, engulfs my tongue, and kisses me deep. I never want his mouth to leave mine. Please don't stop. I want to be stuck in this moment like a black and white photograph. I want people to stop and wonder about the colour of our clothes and what electricity feels like.

We stop to come up for air. My face is flushed and I feel faint. Tired but awake. High but naturally elated. I wish I could die right here like this.

My eyes are blinking rapidly and Francois has been saying my name for a couple of minutes, *"Flora, Flora. Are you okay?"*

"Oh, yeah, yeah...sorry, I'm great..."

I smile at him and I realize I haven't smiled in weeks.

"I shouldn't do drugs," I tell him.

"You could try drinking," he suggests.

"Oh, I drink. Let me tell you."

"I bet you do," he insists.

"No, you don't get it. I don't just drink, I am a professional drinker."

He laughs and then attempts to dispute my credibility.

"Do you get paid to drink?"

"I am deeply offended by this line of questioning; I want to speak to my lawyer."

I'm starting to think he needs to take a walk. Getting bored of this conversation, I ignore his ramblings as I take this moment to run around in circles.

"Gawd almighty I am high!" I shout, flapping my wings, "ah-kah, ah-kah!"

Suddenly, I'm a seagull.

I turn to see Francois laughing, "look, I don't need to prove myself to you. I know all. I see all. I am all! *I am God!* Everyone and their mothers can bow down. And if the day comes where I no longer want to be God, I'll just go back to being a witch!"

Ditching the dude, I look to the water and feel this strong urge to get clean. Not from the drugs but actually clean. I'm trying to recall the last time I felt water actually touch my body; the last time I actually took a shower. It must have been days ago.

I walk towards the water with such wild abandon.

I'm suddenly startled by a flashback of Gypsy telling me to *"walk until I see the tide break."* Whoa. Could she really have predicted I would come to the beach today?

My long flowing skirt drags along the sand. Absorbed by the water's resolve, I let out a yelp from the ice cold on my skin. My skirt buoys along the surface as I try to force myself forward. Not wanting the weight of my clothes to weigh me down, I take everything off, including my thong that's floating behind me. With the water now cool on my breasts, I am set free! How come I never thought of doing this before. It's so natural. And it's way cheaper than paying the water bill.

10:10 AM

Floating along without a care in the world, not sure whether I should swallow the entire lake or not, I accidently end up facing the sun and look directly into its gaze.

"Help, I've gone blind!"
Then my eyes successfully adjust, and I thank the heavens for I have been saved.

The cold is getting to me with it rushing up and down my spine. I can see my hands are just beginning to wrinkle, reminding me it only feels like summer. It's time to wade back towards the shore before I freeze. A few moments of vertigo pass before I am even able to stand.

Just as I'm about to get up to face the world, it suddenly occurs to me that I'm naked.

Great, this makes me feel like I should sink to the bottom with embarrassment as I watch my clothes float halfway across the lake.
"Goodbye clothes," I whisper them away with regret.

At least I still have my jacket. Attempting to slowly inch towards my only piece of dry clothing on land, something feels amiss.

I can feel the gaze of someone staring. Great, just when I thought nobody was around, I am as naked as a grape on a vine. Hesitant to move, I try covering myself with my hands, hoping he'll take a hint and look away.

I can still feel his gaze. I'm officially scared. I'm literally frozen in fear.

I plunge towards my jacket and try to run as fast as I can, draping the jacket around me. But without even thinking, I end up doing the one thing you're never supposed to do.... I look back.

It was one of those quick reactions that couldn't be stopped. I looked and then started to run. But before I knew it, I heard him call my name.

"Flora!"

Uh oh, he knows who I am.

Before I take a second glimpse, it hits me. This strange man looks awfully familiar. He's holding a kite in one hand and the milkcrate in the other.

"How stupid am I?"

Don't answer that.

"How is he even here?"

I slow my pace. My heart stops racing. And I'm instantly struck with mild contempt.

It was him.

It was Patrick.

He appeared mystified by me standing there as well, glimpsing upon my outline like it was the first time he's seen me naked.

"Flora, what are you doing? It's too cold to be swimming, you're gonna get sick."

He wraps his arms around me in a warm embrace.

"What am I doing here? What are you doing here? Before we even answer one another, we both take a second to get warm. He gives me his long johns under his jeans, and then we resumes the conversation.

I am speechless.

He tries to cut the tension, "I was just thinking about

you this morning when I got a text from a friend with all my stuff at their door," he says, rubbing his hands up and down my arms.

"Yeah, that was me. I can explain, but honestly, I'm just so high right now, Patrick…"

A laughing fit takes over my body.
He appears to be staring but I'm not sure why. He could be thinking he needs to take me to the psych ward for all I know.

He's now holding me tightly to his chest and we're both at a loss for words.

"So how come you left it at Florence's?" he asks, referring to the milk crate.

"Um, well, I guess I'm not sure."
"I figured you'd just toss it in the lake or something," he jokes like he can read my mind.

"Me? I would never…"

"I also saw your little birthday gift along with the heartfelt note you left. Only you can use *fuck* in a sentence so eloquently. You've got a real way with words, you know."

"Thank you," I reply.

As for right now, the only thing I want to think about is going home.

Patrick, seeing how tired I am, speaks up, "let's get going."

Linking arms, we walk towards Queen to fetch a cab.

"Fine, let's go," I utter under my breath, "this walk is finally done."

Patrick waves us over a taxi, I consider for a second turning around and running the opposite way, but then it hits me just how tired I am. The taxi pulls up to the curb and I hear Patrick negotiate a fare, "thanks for stopping, how much to get us down the street?"

We get into the car, a hint of tobacco lines the air, and I'm not sure what to think as I listen to Patrick and the driver engage in a conversation about the weather. It looks like it's about to pour, good thing I got in.

Now, dozing in and out of consciousness, I'm no longer able to contemplate any more words. I watch the rain hit the glass, and within seconds, my eyes begin to close, my head gently tilts—falling asleep on Patrick's shoulder without an ounce of regret.

The meter reads eleven dollars.

The time is 11:11 am.

$A = \pi r^2$ 11 x 11   11 x 11 $A = \pi r^2$